IN THE NIGHT KITCHEN

MAURICE SENDAK

HARPER COLLINS PUBLISHERS

FOR SADIE AND PHILIP

DID YOU EVER HEAR OF MICKEY, HOW HE HEARD A RACKET IN THE NIGHT

AND FELL THROUGH THE DARK, OUT OF HIS CLOTHES

PAST THE MOON & HIS MAMA & PAPA SLEEPING TIGHT

AND THEY PUT THAT BATTER UP TO BAKE

A DELICIOUS MICKEY-CAKE.

BUT RIGHT IN THE MIDDLE
OF THE STEAMING
AND THE MAKING
AND THE SMELLING
AND THE BAKING
MICKEY POKED THROUGH
AND SAID:

He kneaded and punched it and pounded and pulled

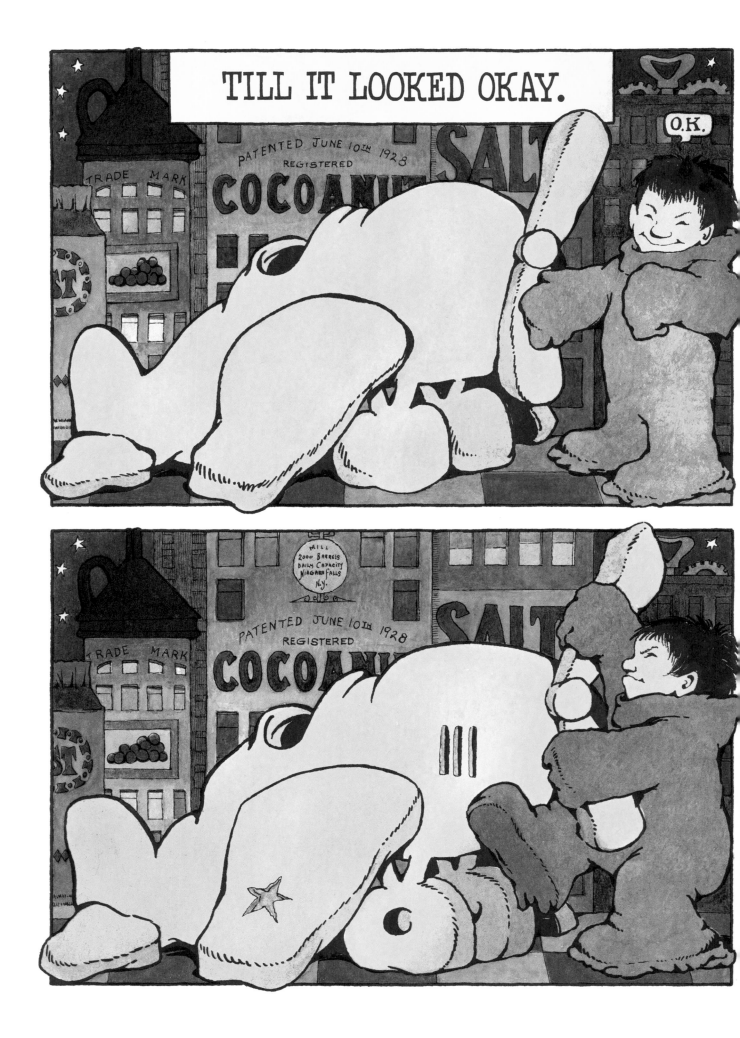

WHEN THE BAKERS RAN UP
WITH A MEASURING CUP, HOWLING:

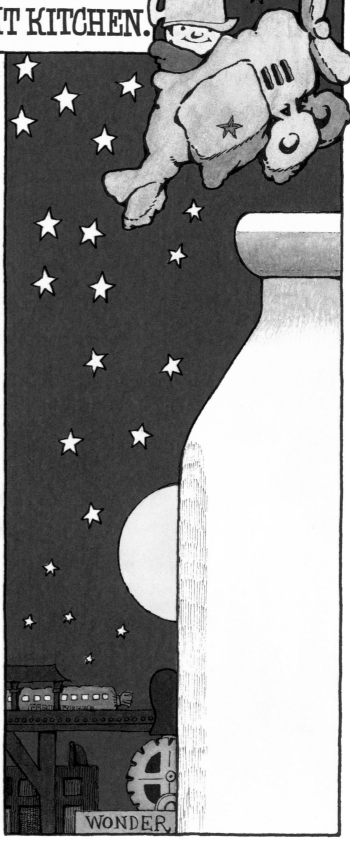

AND OVER THE TOP
OF THE MILKY WAY
IN THE NIGHT KITCHEN.

COCK
·a·
DOODLE
DOO!